Thanks
for Nothing!

a *little* ∧ **BRUCE BOOK** by

#1 *NEW YORK TIMES* BEST-SELLING AUTHOR

RYAN T. HIGGINS

DISNEP • HYPERION

Los Angeles   New York

The air is crisp, and the leaves are changing.

It is fall in Soggy Hollow, and everyone is thankful.

Even Bruce.

He is making a surprise
fall feast for the mice.

There is a surprise for Bruce, too.

"Thanks for the foot bath,"
says Thistle.

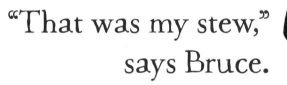

"That was my stew,"
says Bruce.

There are more surprising surprises.

"Thanks for the
crunchy apples,"
says Nibbs.

"Those were for my pie," says Bruce.

"And thanks for
the pumpkins!"
says Rupert.

"Those were for
my other pie,"
says Bruce.

Uh-oh.

The surprises are stacking up.

What will be next?

Wet moose?!

Wait.
Who let the wet moose in here?

Speaking of dinner,
it is time to eat.

But . . . there is no stew.
No pie. No other pie.
No peas.
No gravy.
No potatoes.
No cranberry sauce.
No plates.
No tablecloth.

No nothing.

"What's for dinner?"
asks Thistle.

"Nothing," grumbles Bruce.

Well that IS a surprise . . .

. . . but it was still a fun day.

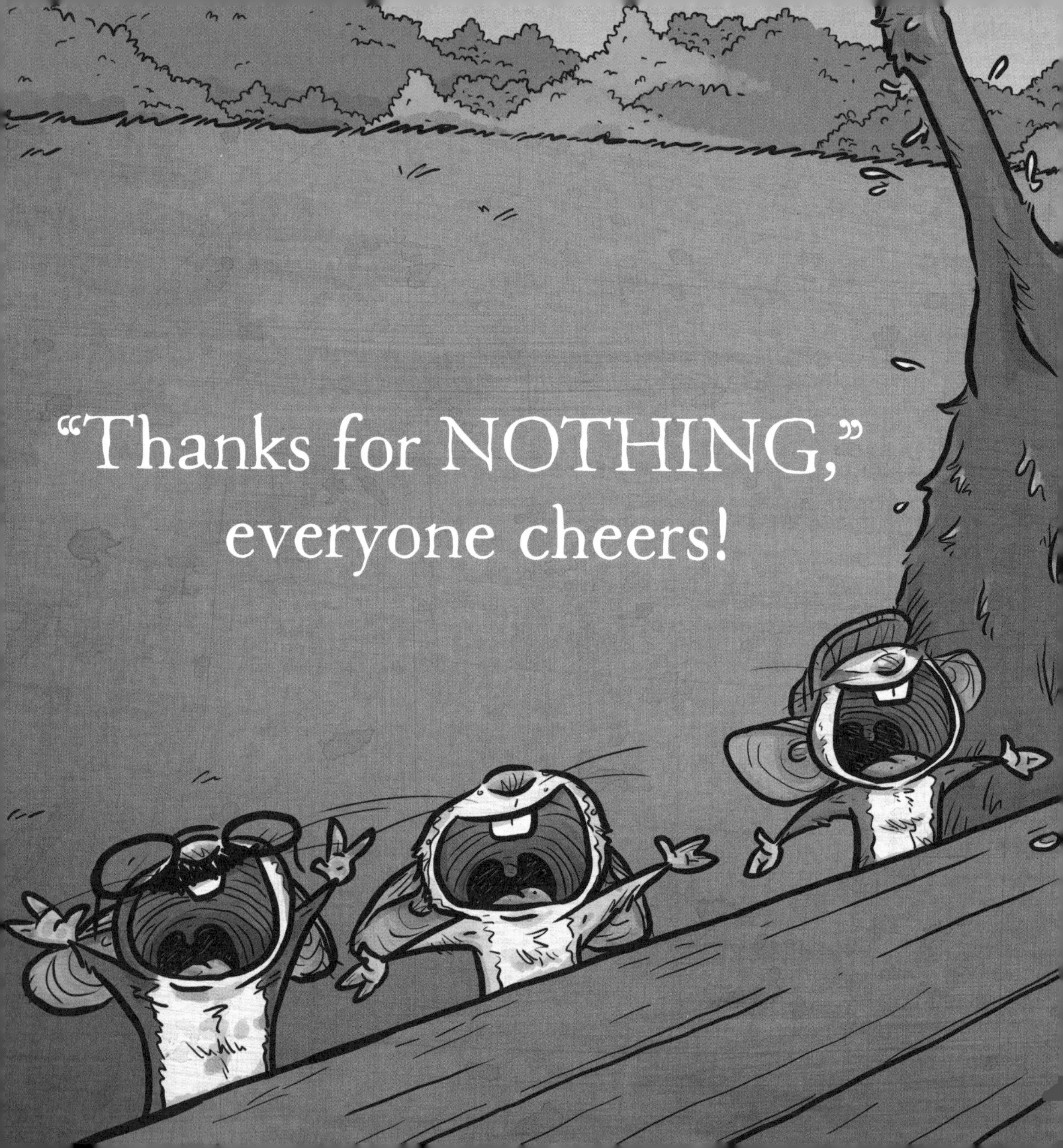

"Thanks for NOTHING,"
everyone cheers!

Sigh...

"You're welcome," says Bruce.